The Christmas Pea Coat

Christmas Pea Coat

WRITTEN BY Richard H. Schneider

ILLUSTRATED BY Higgins Bond

ideals children's books™
Nashville, Tennessee

ISBN 0-8249-5474-2

Published by Ideals Children's Books
An imprint of Ideals Publications
A division of Guideposts
535 Metroplex Drive, Suite 250
Nashville, Tennessee 37211
www.idealsbooks.com

Color separations by Precision Color Graphics, Franklin, Wisconsin

Printed and bound in Italy

Library of Congress Cataloging-in-Publication Data

Schneider, Richard H., 1922-
  The Christmas pea coat / written by Richard H. Schneider ; illustrated by
Higgins Bond.
      p. cm.
  Summary: On Christmas Eve in snow-covered Boston, Henry Chance
invites the school bully Buck O'Grady to dinner at his home and learns a
lesson in giving.
  ISBN 0-8249-5474-2 (alk. paper)
  [1. Christmas—Fiction. 2. Sharing—Fiction. 3. Bullies—Fiction. 4. Boston
(Mass.)—History—Fiction.] I. Bond, Higgins, ill. II. Title.
  PZ7.S36425Ch 2004
  [E]—dc22
                                2004004200

Designed by Eve DeGrie

10 9 8 7 6 5 4 3 2 1

He who has two coats,
let him give to him who has none.

IT WAS CHRISTMAS EVE

and snowflakes floated down over all of Boston. Some settled on top of the Bunker Hill Monument. Others swirled around the steeple of the Old North Church. And quite a few landed on the shoulders of young Henry Chance, who was happily walking home to his family's Christmas dinner.

Henry was coming home from the Christmas Eve service at his church. He'd had to hurry after his paper route to make the service on time, but now he jangled the quarters and half-dollars that he'd collected from the newspaper subscribers. With the two dollars and seventy-five cents he'd collected tonight, along with the three-and-a-half dollars he had at home, in six or seven months, he'd have enough money for that pea coat—something he had always wanted. The very thought of a navy blue sailor's jacket warmed him in the icy weather of the night.

When Henry turned a corner, a chill came over him. On the street before him lived Buck O'Grady, the school bully. Buck was a grade behind Henry, but he was much bigger and he loved to pick on kids. He was strong, strong enough to pick up almost any boy by his feet and shake the coins out of his pockets.

Henry trembled as he looked down the dark street. He knew his money would soon disappear if the bully found him. If he took the longer way around, he would be late for Christmas dinner. He thought of the savory goose his mother was cooking, her sweet potatoes glazed with maple syrup, the pumpkin pies. His heart rose at the thought of his mother, father, sisters, and brothers, and Uncle Charles–all of them sitting around the table singing, joking, and having a very good time.

He lifted his chin and started down Buck O'Grady's street. The snow was deeper now. He was glad that his footsteps hardly made a sound.

Then he heard something. Soft music sounded across the snow-covered fences. It was "Silent Night." Someone was outside singing in the darkness.

Suddenly Henry was filled with terror. The singing was coming from Buck O'Grady's stoop. And judging from its rasping sound, it must be Buck himself! Everybody knew Buck's mother worked nights, and he had no father. So this was Buck's Christmas, singing alone into the night.

Something touched Henry's
heart. He turned toward the boy on
the stoop. The singing stopped.

"What do you want?" Buck
snarled.

Henry swallowed hard before he
answered. "Hey, Buck, uh . . . uh,
how about coming to our house for
Christmas dinner?" There, he had
said it. He waited for Buck to launch
himself from the stoop and hit him.

Instead there was silence. Then,
with a catch in his voice, Buck said,
"Naw, got an invitation up the
street."

Henry knew he was bluffing.

"What's the matter?" Henry said. "You afraid?"

"Afraid?" Buck shouted. "I'll show you who's afraid!" He leaped off the stoop and hurled a snowball at Henry.

Henry ducked and threw one back.

"Ha! You missed!" Buck laughed.

The two went running down the street, pelting each other as they went. Huffing and puffing, they arrived at Henry's house.

Suddenly Buck was quiet. "You think it's all right?"

"Sure," Henry said. He pushed open the kitchen door and they stepped into a bright, warm room full of mouth-watering smells of roasted goose and spicy pumpkin pies.

Henry's mother looked up from the oven. "You're just in time for dinner," she said. In Henry's house there was always room for one more.

Buck stood wide-eyed. Henry nudged him into the dining room and they took their seats with the rest of the family. Henry's father said the blessing. "Thank you, Lord, for your bounty, for our family, and for the wonderful gift you have given us this night in the form of your Son."

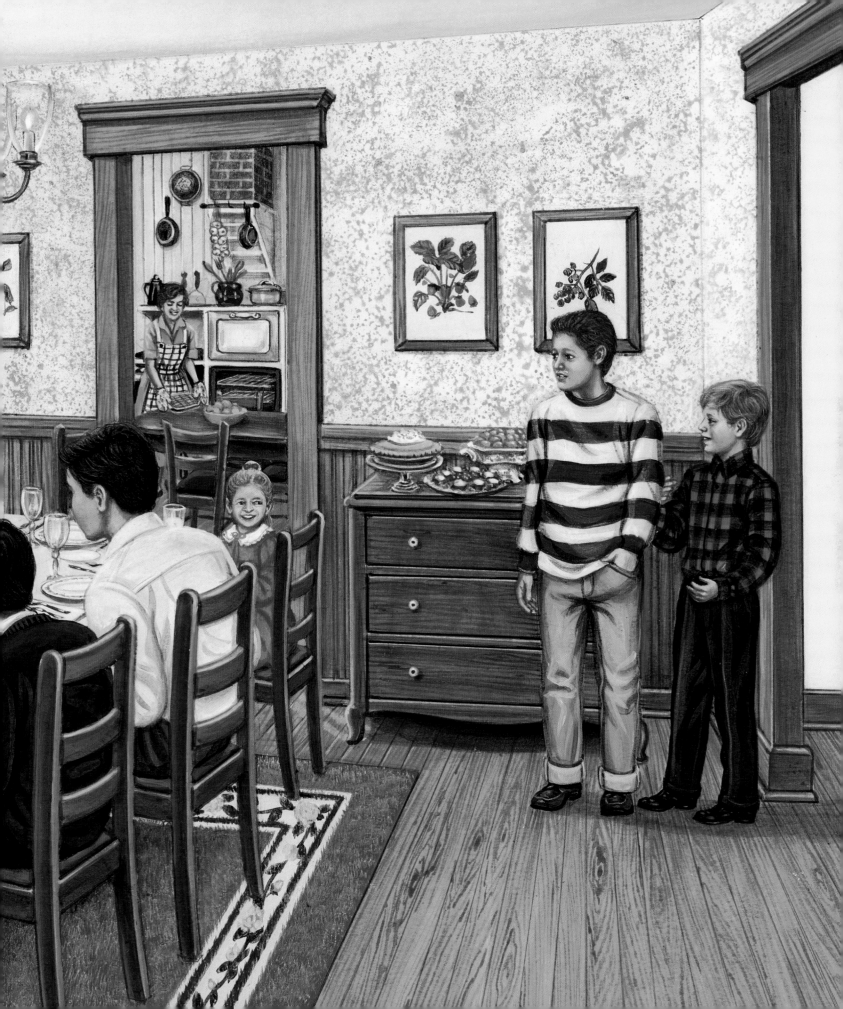

Henry looked up in time to see
something glimmer on Buck's cheek.
Everyone passed steaming potatoes,
cranberries, and slices of goose again
and again, while laughing and talking.
Uncle Charlie's voice boomed as he
told about Christmases he had spent at
sea. He looked over at Henry.

"Another few years and you'll be
out there with me, Lad!"

"Now, Charles, don't make the boy
grow up any faster than he has to," said
Henry's mother.

"He will when he sees the gift I got
for him this year," laughed his uncle.

Henry wondered if it would be
another one of those coconuts with a
silly face carved on it.

After dinner, they all trooped into the living room, where a tall fir tree stood in a corner. Logs crackled in the fireplace, and soon the room was alive with the singing of carols. When Buck joined in, Henry felt he didn't have such a bad voice after all.

"And now it's time to see what's under the tree," said Mrs. Chance.

The gifts were oranges, a hand-painted china teapot, and a wooden box into which a picture of a sailing ship had been burned with a red-hot needle. Henry noticed Buck in the corner, looking forlorn, and was about to go over to him with a bowl of peppermint balls when Uncle Charles's big voice boomed, "I told you I had something special for you."

Henry stood, hardly able to believe what his uncle was holding out to him—a pea coat, a real pea coat. Not a cheap imitation, but a real seaman's navy blue coat.

Thrilled, Henry slipped on the coat. He looked around the room as the family *oohed* and *aahed.* Then he saw Buck in the corner watching.

Something in Buck's face clutched Henry's heart. It wasn't envy, but a deep hunger for a home where love and laughter flowed, a loving mother and father. Buck didn't even have an uncle. Suddenly, words Henry had heard at the Christmas Eve service echoed in his heart. "He who has two coats, let him give to him who has none."

On this holy night, Henry knew there was one thing he could do. He hunched up so his hands slid up inside the jacket's sleeves. Looking up, he said, "Uh . . . it's great, Uncle Charles, but it's a little big for me."

"Ho!" his uncle laughed. "That's a man's jacket, Henry. You'll grow into it."

Henry looked over at Buck. "Oh, maybe it will fit my friend better. He's much bigger than I."

Uncle Charles was a wise man. "Maybe it will," he said. "Hey, mate," he called. "Let's see if you're man enough to wear this pea coat."

Buck's face lit up. Then he
stopped and looked at Henry.

"Go ahead," Henry urged. "It's
just your size."

Slowly, Buck put on the coat. He
could only mumble a husky "Thanks."

Later, after the fire had burned low, Henry said goodbye
to Buck and watched him walk away in the snow, the flakes
settling on the shoulders of his new pea coat. Standing in the
cold, Henry had never felt so warm, so good, so richly blessed.